Bedtime Stories
TO READ TOGETHER

A gift for:

_____

From:

_____

Published by Hallmark Gift Books,
a division of Hallmark Cards, Inc.,
Kansas City, MO 64141
Visit us on the Web at www.Hallmark.com.

Editor: Jared Smith
Art Director: Kevin Swanson
Designer: Brian Pilachowski
Production Artist: Dan Horton

ISBN: 978-1-59530-425-4
BOK1184

Printed and bound in China
AUG11

Bedtime Stories
TO READ TOGETHER

BY Keely Chace

Introduction   6

Little Red Hopping Hood   8

Jackrabbit and the Beanstalk   14

The Emperor's Moo Clothes   22

Tom Tiny Paw   28

The Princess and the Peanut   36

Pandarella   42

Snowy Fox and the Three Bears   50

The Lonely Pony   56

Introduction

Little owls are lucky, don't you think? After all, they get to stay up all night long!

But if you're reading this, you're not a little owl. You have to go to bed at night, even if you're not feeling tired. Some nights it's hard to fall asleep, especially when you know that right outside your bedroom door, there are adventures to be had and friends to have them with.

The trouble is, you have to get some rest if you want to do all

those fun things tomorrow. So here's a book of stories you can read with someone before you say good night. And when you close the book, your little owl night light can stay on. It will keep shining to remind you that you've got adventures of your own waiting for you tomorrow . . . just on the other side of your dreams.

Little Red Hopping Hood

There once lived a sweet kangaroo joey known for the red cape and hood she always wore. When other animals saw her out and about, they would nudge each other and say, "Look, mate. There goes Little Red Hopping Hood." And the name stuck.

It was the girl's Grandma Sally who had made the cape and hood for her. Grandma Sally loved her granddaughter with all her heart, and it always did her good when the girl came to visit. So when

Little Red Hopping Hood's mother received word that Grandma Sally was sick, she knew just the thing to make her feel better. She packed a basket of food and medicine for Grandma Sally and gave it to Little Red Hopping Hood to take to her.

"Now, mind you go straight there," said Mother. "You don't want to get caught in the open outback in the heat of the afternoon. And don't talk to any strangers. Off you go, then!"

With that, Little Red Hopping Hood bounded off into the dusty red country that led to Grandma Sally's. The sun was not yet very high in the sky, and it was pleasant going. The girl hummed to herself as she hopped along. She had not gone far, however, before someone trotted up alongside her. It was a dingo. (That's a wild dog of the outback, if you didn't know—a big one!) He had a hungry look that Little Red Hopping Hood didn't like one bit. But when he spoke, he seemed to know her, and he sounded friendly enough.

"G'day, Little Red Hopping Hood," said the dingo. "Where are you off to in such a hurry?"

"I'm going to Grandma Sally's," she said. "She's sick and needs cheering up."

The dingo considered this. "What a sweet girl you are, visiting your sick granny. But don't forget to have a little fun of your own along the way. The wildflowers are beautiful this time of year."

Little Red Hopping Hood stopped and looked around. The dingo was right—the flowers *were* pretty. And it *was* early. She could pick a nice bouquet for Grandma Sally and still get there before the day grew hot.

The dingo waved good-bye and left Little Red Hopping Hood bouncing this way and that, picking flowers to her heart's content. When she was out of sight, the dingo broke into a flat run to Grandma Sally's house. Little Red Hopping Hood certainly looked delicious, but with a little patience, he figured he could make a meal of her AND her sick granny. When the dingo got to the house, he burst inside and found Grandma Sally in bed. Before she was half awake, the rude fellow grabbed her, stuffed her into the wardrobe, and locked her inside. Then he helped himself to one of Grandma's nightgowns, her best bonnet, and her reading glasses from the nightstand. He put everything on and climbed into her bed just like he owned it. (Yes, dingoes are like that. They can be nice enough when they want to, but normally, they have no manners at all.)

A short time later, there came a knock at the door. "Grandma Sally? It's me, your Little Red Hopping Hood."

In his best sick granny voice, the dingo said, "The door's open. Please come in, dearie."

Little Red Hopping Hood came inside, set her basket down, and hopped over to the bedside and took Grandma by the paw. Poor Grandma! She didn't look quite herself. Not at all.

"I've brought you some flowers, Grandma," said Little Red Hopping Hood, "and if you don't mind my saying so . . . what big eyes you have today!"

"The better to see you with!" said the dingo, in his phony granny voice.

"And, my! What a big nose you have, too."

"The better to smell you with!" said the dingo, his mouth watering.

"And, wow! What big, sharp teeth you have, Grandma!"

"The better to EAT you with!" snarled the dingo, and he lunged at Little Red Hopping Hood.

At that very moment, a boomer happened to be passing by Grandma Sally's house. (A boomer is a boy kangaroo, if you didn't know—a big one!) Hearing the ruckus, the boomer burst inside and found the dingo going for Little Red Hopping Hood. The boomer edged between them and delivered a massive kick, sending the dingo yelping out the front door with his tail between his cowardly legs.

"G'day, then!" the boomer called after the fleeing dingo.

"Thanks for the hand!" said Little Red Hopping Hood. "Or the foot, I guess I should say."

"No problem, Miss," said the boomer. "Always happy to give a dingo a lesson in manners."

Just then, the two of them heard a tapping from inside the wardrobe. They unlocked it, and there was Grandma Sally, sick but already feeling better at the sight of her granddaughter's face. Little Red Hopping Hood stayed with Grandma a few days until she was all better. And from that day on, the little joey in the red hood was careful to do exactly as her mother said and never to talk to any dingoes, no matter how friendly they seemed.

Jackrabbit and the Beanstalk

Long ago, in a dry desert country, there lived a poor jackrabbit and his mother in a little adobe hut. The two of them had nothing to live on but prickly pears and the milk from their old Nanny goat, but as the dry years wore on, Nanny ate up the very last blade of green grass in sight. Jack and his mother had nothing else to feed her, so Jack went to sell old Nanny for whatever they could get. Jack's mother knew they wouldn't get much for her, but she certainly expected more than the pawful of beans Jack returned with.

"You traded Nanny for a few beans?" she said furiously. "In case you haven't noticed, we're in the middle of a desert! How are we supposed to make beans grow, Jack?"

"Oh, but you don't understand, mother. These are magic beans," said Jack. "The old tarantula told me so."

"You traded Nanny to a tarantula? Oh, Jack, how could you be so foolish?" And with that, she snatched the beans from Jack's paw and tossed them out the window.

Jack and his mother went to bed early, with no milk to drink and not a bite to eat. That night, lightning flashed, thunder boomed, and it rained for the first time years. When Jack awoke the next morning, he looked out the window and found that a giant beanstalk had sprouted up overnight! Having no breakfast to eat, and nothing better to do, Jack went outside and started climbing the beanstalk. He climbed it right up into the clouds, until he reached a strange-looking land in the sky, full of towering scrub and the tallest cacti he had ever seen. Jack hopped about cautiously, hippity-tippity. After a time, he came to the largest house he had ever seen. Jack had nothing to lose, so he knocked at the door. He was more than a little surprised when a giant black-and-gold butterfly answered.

"Hi there, little jackrabbit," said the butterfly. "It's not safe for you here. You'd better hop back to where you came from."

"Please, ma'am," said Jack, "may I have something to eat? I haven't eaten in days."

The thing about butterflies, even giant ones, is that they are very kindhearted. This giant butterfly felt sorry for poor Jack, so she let him in and fed him bread and honey. Jack sat on top of an enormous table and had almost finished his tasty snack when the house began to tremble and shake. *Thud! Thud! Thud!* went the table as a set of heavy footsteps approached.

"Oh, no! There comes my master!" said the butterfly. "Quick! Hide in here!"

Jack obediently climbed into the oven, where he could just see out through a small crack in its door. Then the front door of the house opened, and in came a giant coyote! Now, Jack was plenty scared of normal-size coyotes, so you can imagine how he felt about this one.

The coyote sat and sniffed the air. Then he said:

Fee-fi-fo-fouse!
I smell a jackrabbit in my house!
High or low, there or here,
I'll catch him by his bunny ear!

"Don't be silly," said the butterfly to the coyote. "It's just your imagination. Here, have some bread and honey."

The giant coyote wasn't so sure about that, but he was very hungry. He came to the table and ate, but all the while, he kept sniffing around, trying to find where the jackrabbit scent was coming from.

After he ate, the coyote said, "Butterfly! Bring me my gold." (That's right. Coyotes, even giant ones, are lazy and won't do anything for themselves if they can help it.)

The butterfly was anxious to get Jack out of the house without any trouble, so she brought the coyote his pouch of gold coins, even though it was very heavy for her. The colossal coyote started counting out his gold, but he was not so good at counting, and the effort soon wore him out.

"One, two . . . five . . . eleven . . ." he counted. Then the coyote's voice trailed off, and he laid down his head and started snoring.

"Now's your chance!" the big butterfly whispered to Jack. "Run!

Hop! Just go!"

Jack crawled out of the oven and, just as he was about to make his escape, leaped up onto the table and snatched one of the coyote's huge gold coins. After hearing the overgrown mutt count, Jack was sure he would never miss it. Then Jack hopped out of the house and back to the beanstalk as fast as he could, though it wasn't easy with the big coin to carry. When Jack reached the beanstalk, he dropped down the coin and then climbed down after it.

As you might have guessed, Jack's mother forgave him about the beans when she saw the enormous piece of gold. They ate like desert kings for weeks on all the food they were able to buy with it. But eventually their cupboards grew bare once more, and the desert nights grew cold against their thin blankets. Jack knew what he had to do. He climbed the beanstalk up into the clouds and went again to the house of the giant coyote.

"What are you doing back here?" asked the butterfly when she saw Jack.

Jack shivered. "Please, ma'am. I'm chilled to the bone, and it seems so cozy in there. May I come in and warm my ears for a while?"

The kind butterfly couldn't stand to see anyone shiver, so, against her better judgment, she invited him in again. The coyote's house was steamy warm from the mammoth bucket of laundry the butterfly was washing for her master. It would have made a nice swimming pool for Jack, who sat right next to it, warming his stiff paws. He was just getting really comfy when the house began to tremble in a familiar way. *Thud! Thud! Thud!* went the paddle in the laundry bucket. The butterfly gestured for Jack to hide in the corner behind the bucket, which he did—and not a moment too soon!

The coyote burst through the door and sniffed the air. Then he said:

Fee-fi-fo-fail!
I smell a jackrabbit's fluffy tail!
He steals my gold! He eats my honey!
I don't like that kind of bunny!

"There you go chasing imaginary rabbits again," said the butterfly. "You must have had a hard day. Why don't you lie down? I just put on fresh sheets and blankets."

The giant coyote wasn't so sure the smell was imaginary, but he was very tired. He went to his bed and lay down, but he kept sniffing around for the jackrabbit scent.

After a while, the coyote said, "Butterfly! Bring me my guitar."

Eager to soothe him, the butterfly brought him the guitar. It was normal in size and looked just like any other guitar to Jack, but then it did something other guitars don't often do.

"Play!" the coyote commanded.

And the guitar played—all by itself! It strummed the saddest, sweetest lullaby Jack had ever heard, and gradually the coyote was overcome by the soothing music and the coziness of his bed. He started snoring, and the butterfly motioned for Jack to seize this chance to leave. Jack emerged from his corner, but before leaving, he used his powerful hind legs to leap up on the coyote's bed. Jack snatched the guitar and hopped for his life out the door. Luckily, the guitar kept right on playing its lullaby, and the coyote kept right on snoring.

Jack carried the guitar down the beanstalk and brought it to his mother, who was thrilled with what it could do. Soon, animals started coming from far and wide to see it, and they paid to hear its sweet music, which sounded even sweeter now that it was away from the bossy coyote. Jack and his mother used the money they earned to buy food, thick blankets, and wood for their stove.

The guitar's music never seemed to run out, and Jack and his mother lived in comfort for the first time in their lives. There was no need to climb the beanstalk again, but for some reason, Jack couldn't stop thinking about it. He liked that big pretty butterfly! He hated to think of her slaving away for a giant coyote who couldn't even count. Jack decided he would visit her again.

This time, when Jack knocked at the coyote's door, he didn't look so poor or pitiful, but the butterfly let him in for old times' sake.

"Come away with me!" said Jack, nibbling on a giant cookie the butterfly had just made.

"It sounds nice, but my master would never let me go," said the butterfly. "He needs me to make his bed, bake him cookies, bring his gold . . . He can't do anything for himself."

"Well, it's time he learned," said Jack. "Come on! Let's go before he comes home!"

So Jack hopped and the butterfly flew out the door and toward the beanstalk. But before they were halfway there, the ground began to tremble and shake behind them.

The coyote was giving chase—and he was gaining on them. *Whew!* Jack could smell the coyote's monstrous breath as it growled these words:

Fee-fi-fo-fum!
Look out, jackrabbit, here I come!
Leap and hop! By and by,
I'll take back my butterfly!

Jack slid down the beanstalk, and the big butterfly flew circles around it on her way to the ground below. When Jack reached the ground, he looked up to see the big coyote taking his first uncertain step onto the beanstalk.

"Here!" said the butterfly, bringing Jack an ax that had been leaning against the hut. Jack chopped at the beanstalk for all he was worth. When the coyote noticed the chopping, he howled angrily and scrambled back up the beanstalk and into the clouds. A moment later, the beanstalk gave a creak and fell to the ground with a crash.

Jack and his mother lived happily from that day on, with the magic guitar, full cupboards, and warm blankets for cold nights. Jack told the giant butterfly to fly free and see the world, which she did, but she often came back to visit . . . because she liked that brave little jackrabbit! Whenever she came, Jack took care to show her the same kindness she had shown him in that giant land in the sky.

The Emperor's Moo Clothes

Once upon a very silly time, in a land of great green farms, there reigned a vain cow emperor who owned closets and closets full of clothes. He admired himself for having great fashion sense, and he worked hard at it. He could spend whole days just trying on his fancy outfits and looking at himself in the mirror. All his trousers and waistcoats were works of art. But it was the emperor himself who was truly a piece of work. He had learned as a young ruler that it wasn't easy running an empire and being stylish at the same time. And that's why he mostly just focused on being stylish.

One day, a pair of crafty crows came to the palace and requested an audience with the emperor. Normally, the imperial minister would not have interrupted the emperor's private fashion show for a meeting with a couple of crows, but these two said they had some fabulous new cloth that the emperor just *had* to see. The emperor was annoyed by the interruption, but he was also curious. He dressed himself in an impressive suit of royal purple and went to receive the visitors.

The two crows bowed low when the emperor entered the room. "Your Excellency," they said together. "Masters Rip and Fleece, fine weavers and tailors, at your service."

"Welcome!" said the emperor. "What's this I hear about some new cloth you have to show me?"

"Oh, yes!" said Rip. "But it's not just any new cloth . . ."

"It's MOO cloth!" said Fleece. "The finest cloth in the world!"

"Only those with real fashion sense can appreciate its quality," Rip added.

"Only those with genuine good taste can see how extraordinary it is," said Fleece.

Rip made a show of turning around and pretending to pull something from his bag. "Are you ready, Your Excellency?" Then he turned to the emperor with his wings outstretched. "Here it is. *Ta-dah!*"

"Well, it's simply magnificent! What marvelous texture! What a wonderful color!" the emperor gushed. "I must have a suit of Moo clothes immediately. Spare no expense—just make me some Moo clothes."

The crows grinned and bowed low again, promising to begin immediately. They set up a loom in the emperor's barn. Day after day, they asked the emperor to pay them for thread, fabric dye, and many other supplies needed for making Moo cloth. And day after day, they toiled over their invisible work. No one could see the threads they spun, or the color of the cloth they seemed to be weaving, but the crows sure made a convincing show of it.

When the imperial minister came to check on their work, Rip and Fleece asked him if he liked the pattern they had chosen for the Moo cloth. And weren't the new colors rich and fine? The minister didn't actually know, because the minister couldn't actually *see* any pattern, or color, or any cloth at all, for that matter. He decided then and there that he must have had poor fashion sense his whole life and never known it until now. Of course, he couldn't risk admitting this to the emperor, so he reported back that the weaving was coming along just beautifully, and that the emperor was going to love his Moo clothes. The emperor was thrilled to hear it, and he did what anyone in that situation would do: he scheduled a big parade so that he could show off his Moo clothes to everyone in town.

One morning, after many weeks of work, Rip and Fleece made a big production of cutting the cloth from their loom. They proceeded to cut and sew a suit of clothes from the cloth. What style was the shirt? What length was the coat? What color were the britches? No one could say. Whatever the case, the Moo clothes appeared to take a lot of flashy needle threading and stitching. But at last, the crows finished their work. With much ceremony, they presented the long-awaited Moo clothes to the emperor. Everyone held their breath as the emperor inspected them.

The emperor smiled. "These Moo clothes are even finer than I hoped! Let me go put them on!"

The emperor went to his chamber to dress and admire himself in his mirrors. After a while, he returned to the throne room, and everyone applauded and complimented him on his Moo clothes. The emperor enjoyed this immensely. He was ready for his parade.

The emperor marched proudly beneath a purple canopy.

Behind him walked several servants, ready to adjust his coat or tie if ever he should need them to. The road was lined with the emperor's subjects, who cheered and shouted flattering things about the Moo clothes and the emperor's fine fashion sense. All of them seemed to be impressed—all except for a single small calf.

As the emperor passed, the calf tugged at her mother's ear. "Mama, mama," she said, "why is everyone talking about the emperor's Moo clothes? It looks to me like the emperor isn't wearing ANY clothes!"

Others overheard the calf's observation, and the rumor began to spread through the crowd. The emperor's Moo clothes were no clothes at all! The emperor wasn't wearing anything!

Eventually, the rumor reached the ears of the emperor himself. But after careful consideration, he did what anyone in that situation would do: he kept right on marching. After all, what did all these common cows know about fashion?

Tom Tiny Paw

Once upon a time, there lived seven kitten brothers—Boots, Mittens, Tiger, Fluffy, Sammy, Ozzy, and Tom. Because Tom was the youngest of the litter, and the smallest by far, his mother and brothers affectionately called him Tom Tiny Paw. The brothers sometimes teased Tom about being so small, but they also admired him for being very clever. Everyone knows that curious kitten brothers can get into plenty of mischief, and most of the time it

was Tom Tiny Paw's cleverness that got them back out of it.

One day, the kittens were out playing in the woods. They were having so much fun that they plum forgot to go home before dark. Night fell around them, and the kittens soon became lost. Even with cat eyes that could see in the dark, nothing looked the same to them. The familiar trees they had climbed and played in during the day now seemed strange and scary. Even clever Tom could not find the well-known landmarks that should have led them quickly home.

"We're lost!" said Boots, who was starting to cry.

"I want my supper," Mittens whined.

"I'm afraid we're going to *be* supper," said Tiger.

"Don't be ninnies," said Fluffy. "Tom will get us home, won't you, Tom?"

"Well, I can't be sure of the way," said Tom, "but look! There's a light over there. Either it's home, or it's a safe place for us to stay until morning."

So Tom led his brothers toward the light. It turned out to be much farther away than it had looked at first, but after a long march, they finally came to a cozy-looking cabin with a warm glow coming from the windows. It was a sight for sore kitten eyes after the long walk in the cold dark woods.

"Hooray for Tom!" said Sammy.

"Do you think they'll feed us supper?" asked Ozzy.

"Only one way to find out," said Tom.

Tom knocked at the cabin door, and someone motherly answered. The kittens were missing their own mama pretty badly by this time, and they should have been glad to see a motherly face. But this motherly face was that of a very big dog, which made the kittens nervous.

"What have we here?" asked the mama dog. "Seven kittens all alone in the woods at night? Your mother must be worried sick."

"We got lost," said Tom.

"Well, in that case, you'd better stay here for the night," said the mama dog. "It's not safe for little kittens to be out alone this late."

The kittens weren't exactly convinced it would be much safer inside a dog's cabin, but at least it would be warm, and maybe there would be supper. Brave little Tom went in, and his brothers followed him. Once all the kittens were inside, the mama dog fussed and fawned over them, and fed them all saucers of milk. With full bellies, the six older brothers grew quite dull and sleepy, but Tom was careful to keep his sharp wits about him. After supper, the mama dog put the kittens to bed in a small room with her seven sleeping puppies. Boots, Mittens, Tiger, Fluffy, Sammy, and Ozzy fell asleep quickly, but Tom stayed awake, listening. He overheard the mama dog talking to herself in the next room, and this is what he heard her say:

"Oh, how surprised and pleased my puppies will be when they wake up and find new kittens to play with! And there are seven of them—one for each. My darlings will be so excited!"

New kittens to play with? What!?! Had the puppies worn out their last batch of kittens? Tom cringed at the thought of clumsy puppy feet, puppy slobber, and, worst of all, puppy breath! *Ewww!,* It was too awful. Tom knew he and his brothers had to get away by morning, so with his clever little mind, he thought up an escape plan.

Tom waited until he heard the mama dog start to snore. Then he took his own and his brothers' caps and tiptoed silently over to the puppies' bed. One by one, Tom switched the kittens' caps with the puppies' night bonnets. When he returned to bed, he put a bonnet on himself and one on each of his brothers. When the first morning light shined through the bedroom curtains, Tom woke his brothers and motioned for them to be quiet and follow him. The kittens had to tiptoe right past the mama dog on their way to the front door. They were as quiet as they could be, but still, the watchful mama dog stirred from her slumber as they passed. In her half-awake state, all she noticed were seven little figures in bonnets going outside. Assuming it was her puppies going out to potty, the mama dog went back to sleep.

After the brothers were outside, with the door shut safely behind them, Boots whispered, "What's wrong? Why did you wake us up so early, Tom?"

"That mama dog wants us to play with her puppies!" said Tom.

"*Ewww!* Puppy breath!" said Mittens.

"Exactly," said Tom. "Now, let's go!"

The kittens hurried away, but it wasn't long before the mama dog woke up all the way, only to find her puppies still asleep in their bed, and the kittens all gone. Now, cats may not think dogs are terribly smart, but this mama dog understood right away that she had been tricked by a bunch of kittens. *Oooh!* Was she ever mad! She burst out the front door, determined to get back her puppies' new playmates.

The mama dog was a good hunter, and she quickly picked up the kittens' scent. Her stride was much longer than that of the kittens, and she had them in her sights quicker than you can say kitty litter.

Fluffy spotted her first. "Don't look now, brothers, but we have company!"

Of course, they all looked back anyway and saw the mama dog steadily gaining on them. In another minute at most she would catch up with them. Tom knew he needed to think of something fast. He looked around and was surprised to find that he knew where he was. He had been to this part of the woods before. Suddenly, he took a sharp left turn, and his brothers followed him. The mama dog turned after them and kept coming closer and closer. The kittens could hear her breathing. Then they could feel her hot breath on their tails. The mama dog was almost on top of them when Tom led his frightened brothers right over the edge of a sheer cliff. The fall was no problem for little kittens, who can easily land on their feet, but the drop was much too steep and risky for a big heavy dog. The kittens landed far below, safe and sound, and then they looked up and waved at the mama dog high above.

"Thanks for looking out for us last night!" called Tiger.

"You've been most kind!" yelled Sammy.

"Maybe we can play with your puppies some other time!" said Ozzy.

"Not likely," said Tom under his breath. " 'Bye now!"

The disappointed mama dog barked at the kittens, but she knew she'd never catch them now, so she gave up and turned for home. With Tom to guide them, the kittens soon found their way home, too. Their own mother was overjoyed to see her seven little troublemakers again. She scolded them soundly, but she was too glad to have them back to stay mad at them for long. Over a breakfast of cold tuna, the kittens told her the story of their adventure with the mama dog.

Mama cat shook her head and said, "Well, you deserve to have puppies for playmates. When will you kittens ever learn?"

But Tom Tiny Paw and his brothers didn't answer their mother. They only smiled at each other across the table, thinking of the new adventures they would have right after breakfast.

The Princess
and the Peanut

Alone elephant was crossing the savannah when a wall of dark storm clouds rolled in and started pouring down rain. The young elephant was caught completely by surprise, for the rainy season was not due to begin for days. The miserable creature continued on her way, hoping to find some shelter. Eventually, she came to the gates of a magnificent castle. Perhaps you've never heard of a castle on the African savannah, but it sure was a lucky thing for this wet elephant that there was one. She knocked at the gate, and was amazed when the queen elephant herself opened it.

"Please, your highness," said the young elephant to the queen, "I am a lost princess, with no shelter and no way to reach my family until the rain stops. May I stay in your nice dry castle for the night?"

Now, what would you think if a half-drowned stranger showed up at your door saying she was a princess? Would you believe her? Well, the elephant queen didn't believe this soggy stranger, either— not for a second—but she was a kind queen and would have taken in anyone but a hungry lion.

The queen let the young elephant in and handed her over to the care of the head housekeeper, who gave the unexpected guest a room and helped her dry off. The lonely young elephant was invited to dine that evening with the queen and her son, the prince. At dinner, the queen was surprised to find that their guest was really quite beautiful when dry, and that her conversation and manners were delightful. The elephant prince, who was of an age to marry, noticed the mystery guest's beauty, too, and enjoyed talking with her. Before the end of dinner, the queen got an idea in her head. It would probably come to nothing, but what could it hurt to try a little experiment?

The queen instructed the head housekeeper to prepare the guest's bed in a very special way. On the bed frame, the house-keeper placed a single peanut, just as the queen had told her to do. On top of that, her maids piled twenty mattresses and twenty thick quilts and blankets. All stacked up, they made a towering bed fit for a princess! When it came time to sleep, the queen and prince bid their guest good night.

"Pleasant dreams," said the prince.

"I hope your bed is all right for you," said the queen. "Sleep well."

"I'm sure I will," said the lonely elephant. "It looks just heav-enly! Thank you so much. Good night."

The guest closed her door and climbed the tall ladder to reach the top of this unusual bed. Then she lay down and pulled the luxu-rious covers up to her trunk. She was awfully tired and expected to fall asleep immediately, but for some reason, she could not get comfortable. She turned this way and that, trying to find a relax-ing position, but each way she tossed felt worse than the last. She turned onto her side, and something jabbed at her. She tried rolling onto her stomach, but that was no better. She flipped onto her back and her other side, but each way, it felt as if there were a rock digging into her body. Finally, out of sheer exhaustion, she did fall asleep, but she kept waking up all through the night because of the invisible lump that poked and plagued her.

When the pale morning light started to peek through her window, the guest gave up on sleeping. She climbed down, washed and dressed, and went to the great room to wait for everyone else to wake up. Her tired head felt as cloudy as the sky outside. Her entire body felt black and blue. If anything, she was even more miserable than she had been out in the rain that continued to fall.

Much later, the guest joined the queen and prince for a big breakfast. The table was spread with all the things she loved to eat—sweet grasses, fresh fruits, and even her favorite delicacy, peanuts. For some reason, though, the guest couldn't even look at the peanuts. Every time she did, her ears sagged, her trunk flopped, and her body started aching all over again. The queen couldn't help but notice this lack of interest in peanuts, not to mention how weary and bedraggled their guest was looking.

"I don't mean to be rude," said the queen, "but you don't look at all well. Did you sleep all right?"

The guest didn't want to be rude either, but she couldn't tell a lie. "I'm sorry, but no, I didn't," she replied. "I barely slept a wink. All night long, I felt like something in the bed was jabbing and poking at me."

"My dear!" the queen exclaimed. "You really are a princess, aren't you?"

"Yes, I am," said the guest, "but I didn't think you believed me."

The queen smiled kindly. "I do now. Because only a real princess could have felt the peanut I had placed under all those mattresses and blankets you slept on. I'm so sorry to have put you through that. Stay with us again, and I will give you a much better bed."

The princess did stay—clear through the rainy season. By day, she and the prince got to know each other, and at night, she slept like a baby on a bed with one mattress and nothing hiding underneath it. When the rains stopped for good, the queen and prince journeyed on with the princess, until they reached yet another great castle on the savannah—the home of the princess and her family. Soon, the prince and princess were married with the blessings of their families, and their two kingdoms were united.

And what a wedding feast it was! You should have seen all the peanuts.

Pandarella

Once upon a time, in a faraway land, there lived a poor country girl named Pandarella. She had her mother's lovely black-and-white face and her father's kind and gentle heart. The girl was cheerful and hardworking, but sadly, her hard work was not enough to make rice grow in a year with no rain. Pandarella's parents had no choice but to send their daughter away to earn her rice elsewhere.

This is how Pandarella came to live in an elegant house with a widow and her two daughters. The widow asked Pandarella to call her "Auntie" and promised to treat her like her own daughter, but nothing could have been further from the truth. While Auntie's own daughters, Lao and Hu, spent their days admiring themselves in mirrors, eating sweets, and giving orders, Pandarella cooked, washed laundry, and scrubbed floors. Every day it was, "Pandarella, mend my gown. Pandarella, fetch me more dumplings. Pandarella, this . . . Pandarella, that . . ." But all this and more, Pandarella did cheerfully. What's more, she remained as lovely as ever, in spite of her hard life. Do you think Auntie and her daughters liked Pandarella for this? Well, they didn't. Pandarella's sweet nature and beauty only made them more jealous and more obnoxious in the demands they made of her.

Busy as she was, Pandarella found time to befriend the smaller residents of the great house. There were the chatty hens who kept Pandarella company when she sat in the sunshine of the courtyard eating her bowl of rice. There was also the rooster, who didn't stop to talk, but who made her laugh as he pranced about. And then there were the mice who told Pandarella wonderful stories at night as she drifted off to sleep on her bamboo mat.

One day Pandarella was busy making Auntie's bed for the second time (because there had been a wrinkle the first time), when she heard a knock at the door. Pandarella answered it, and was surprised when an imperial messenger handed her an invitation. Pandarella hurried to share it with Lao and Hu, who were lounging on their favorite sofas. The sight of the bright red invitation caught their eyes, and they sat up attentively when Pandarella began to read.

"It says there will be a ball tomorrow night in honor of the crown prince, and every maiden in our household is invited to come," read Pandarella.

The two sisters leaped up and twirled around the floor together at this news. But the very next moment, they started giving orders.

"Pandarella, get my green silk gown ready immediately!" said Lao.

"Pandarella, embroider more flowers on my blue slippers. They are so plain!" said Hu.

"And mine too!" said Lao.

Pandarella agreed to each request, but then held up a paw. "All right, all right, but you must leave me a little time to get ready for the ball, too."

This suggestion made the sisters roar with laughter. "Pandarella at the ball!" snarled Lao. "How ridiculous!"

Well, you might have already guessed this, but those mean and lazy sisters gave Pandarella more and more work to do, and Auntie kept her hopping with extra chores, too. All that day, and the next day as well, Pandarella stitched and sewed and searched and slaved to get Lao and Hu ready for the ball. When it came time to go, the sisters only made fun of Pandarella again.

"Pandarella, are you ready to go?" asked Lao as she walked out the door.

"Is THAT what you're wearing?" called Hu with a laugh.

Pandarella looked down at her tattered work clothes. "I guess I won't be going after all," she said softly.

"What a shame," said Auntie, "but don't worry—we'll tell you all about it in the morning when you bring us our breakfast. Good night."

Pandarella was too weary even to manage a smile as the three of them left. She was also too tired to care about the ball anymore. All she wanted to do was curl up on her little mat and sleep. She doubted if she would even stay awake for the mice's stories.

As it turned out, though, Pandarella's night was not quite over. As soon as the door closed behind Auntie and her daughters, Pandarella noticed a strange golden light in the courtyard. She went out to investigate and was surprised by what she found.

"Hello, Pandarella" said an unusually large goldfish peeking up from the edge of the pond. "I've been watching you, and I've come to get you to the ball."

"But I have nothing to wear and no way to get to the palace," said Pandarella. "Also, you're a fish. How could you get me to the ball?"

"Like this!" said the goldfish. With a flick of his tail, the mysterious light grew brighter, and Pandarella watched, amazed, as the lowly henhouse was transformed into a magnificent golden sedan chair.

"How did you do that?" asked Pandarella.

"No time to explain," answered the fish. "We must find someone to carry your chair."

Then, spying three hens and a proud rooster, the goldfish flicked his tail again, turning them into graceful long-legged cranes—one for each of the sedan's four carrying poles. Pandarella couldn't believe her eyes.

"And now for your gown," said the fish.

He looked at Pandarella a long moment, then flicked his tail again. The golden light grew brighter and swirled around Pandarella. When she looked down, she found her work dress gone, and in its place the most beautiful red silk gown. On her feet were matching slippers, with the most splendid embroidery she had ever seen.

Pandarella no longer felt tired, but instead, full of excitement. "I don't deserve these fine things," she said to the goldfish, "but I'm happy to have them. Thank you."

"No thanks are needed," said the fish, "for these things are only enchantments and will not last. Now climb into your chair and be off, but listen! You must take care to leave the ball early, because at midnight, my magic will wear off."

"I will!" said Pandarella, climbing into the chair. "Good-bye!"

With that, the four cranes whisked her away, out the front gate and into the warm moonlit night. They flew her chair swiftly to the imperial palace, and the most impressive of the cranes (the rooster) escorted her up the steps to the palace doors. Inside, Pandarella's eyes were drawn to the elegantly painted walls and the rainbow of richly colored gowns all around the room. But everyone else's eyes were drawn to the pretty panda maiden in her magnificent red gown and slippers. The ballgoers whispered to each other, asking who she was, but no one seemed to know. They all wanted to meet her, especially one particular person.

Pandarella grew worried when she saw an imperial servant approaching her. Oh, no! Was the magic wearing off already? Or was it so obvious that she was only a poor country panda under her fine clothes? The servant asked her to come with him, but to Pandarella's surprise, he didn't escort her out of the palace. Instead, he led her to the thrones of the emperor and the crown prince.

The prince stood and took Pandarella's paw in his. "Would you do me the honor of dancing with me?" he asked.

Pandarella bowed her head. "It would be my pleasure, your majesty."

The two of them danced that dance and many more. In fact, they were inseparable for the rest of the night. With every step and every word they spoke, the prince fell more in love with the gentle, beautiful panda beside him. The other ballgoers watched with great interest, especially Lao, Hu, and Auntie.

"How lucky she is!" said Lao.

"How beautiful, too!" said Hu.

"Yes, and there's something so familiar about her," said Auntie, but try as she might, she could not place where she had seen that sweet face before.

Pandarella and the prince were talking quietly when the palace clock began to chime twelve. In a panic, Pandarella said she must go, and she ran for the palace doors. The prince called after her, but she didn't stop. She dashed outside, down the palace steps, and in her hurry she lost one of her red slippers. There was no time to go back for it. Pandarella climbed into the waiting sedan and the cranes whisked her away into the night once again. They had not gone far, however, before the wonderful enchantments began to wear off, just as the goldfish had said they would. The sedan chair dropped to the ground with a thud, a rickety henhouse once more. And there was Pandarella in her ragged work dress with her old friends, the chickens. All that was left of the enchantments was the lone red slipper that Pandarella had escaped with. She plucked it off her foot to keep it from becoming soiled in the dirty road and ran home as quickly as she could.

Pandarella smiled to herself over the breakfast trays the next morning, as Lao and Hu talked on and on about the crown prince and the beautiful stranger.

"You should have seen her slip—" Lao started to say, but Auntie interrupted her before she could finish.

"Listen to this!" said Auntie, looking at a notice that had just been delivered. "The crown prince has promised to marry the maiden whose paw fits the slipper left at the ball last night. Lao! Hu! This is your chance. Surely one of you will be able to make it fit."

Pandarella was speechless, but that was just as well, because Lao and Hu started talking plenty, ordering Pandarella to get them dressed, brush their fur, bring their jewels, and so on. Late that afternoon there came a knock at the door. Pandarella answered it, and

Auntie welcomed the three imperial footmen who had come to try the slipper on every maiden in the house. Lao tried it first, but the shape of her paw was all wrong. Hu tried it next, and it almost fit . . . with three of her toes hanging out the side. Finally, the head footman turned to Pandarella and gestured for her to sit and try the slipper.

"Oh, no, no," said Auntie. "That will not be necessary."

Pandarella felt crushed, but then thrilled when the head footman took her paw and led her to a chair anyway. He put the slipper on Pandarella's paw, and here's what happened next: Auntie growled with dismay when she saw that the slipper fit Pandarella perfectly. Now she understood why the beautiful stranger had looked so familiar to her the night before. Lao and Hu were confused, but they understood when Pandarella pulled the matching slipper from the pocket of her dress!

Pandarella was taken to the palace, and in a few weeks' time, she and the crown prince were married. The newlywed couple sent for Pandarella's family, who came to live at the palace and never had to worry about rice or rain again. Because Pandarella was very forgiving, she even took care of her old mistress and her daughters. Lao, Hu, and Auntie, too, were all married to important men of the court. And maybe you can guess how they all lived after that . . .

Snowy Fox
and the Three Bears

Way up north, in a land of snow and ice, there lived a little white arctic fox—Snowy Fox—who loved to snoop around in other animals' things. In that same land, there lived a papa, a mama, and a baby polar bear who didn't like anyone messing in their stuff. Maybe you think this is about to turn into a bad combination.

Well, you're right about that.

One morning the polar bear family sat down in the kitchen of their cozy igloo to enjoy their breakfast of blubber porridge. But *ouch!* The porridge was much too hot to eat. Papa polar bear suggested a walk on the sea ice while their breakfast cooled, so off the bears went.

While they were away, Snowy Fox happened upon the igloo.

She knocked, but finding no one at home, she let herself right in. (Told you she was a snoop.) She had never been in a polar bears' igloo before. This would be fun!

It wasn't long before the little fox smelled something tasty in the kitchen. She went to investigate. Blubber porridge! *Yum!* Her favorite! Snowy Fox sat down before papa polar bear's bowl and took a bite. *Ouch!* It was much too hot. Next, she tried mama polar bear's porridge. *Ewww.* It was too cold. At last, she tried baby polar bear's porridge, and *mmm . . .* it was just right. Snowy Fox ate it all up. Then she opened all the kitchen drawers and cabinets for good measure. Inside, she found bone-handle forks, seal butter, sea salt, and some peppermint tea. What funny things polar bears liked to keep in their kitchens!

Bored with utensils and spices, Snowy Fox went to check out the living room. There she found three chairs. Sitting in chairs! *Yay!* Her favorite! First, Snowy Fox sat in papa polar bear's chair. *Ugh.* It was much too hard. Next, she tried mama polar bear's chair. *Odd.* It was way too squishy. At last, she tried baby polar bear's chair, and *ahhh . . .* it was just right. Snowy Fox rocked back and forth in the wee chair, but sadly, its little legs weren't made for rocking, and the chair broke right underneath her. Well, that was too bad, but never mind. Snowy Fox had just noticed the polar bears' stack of magazines, and she couldn't help herself from flipping through them. *Arctic Times . . . Whale Hunter . . . Igloo Living . . .* what funny things polar bears liked to read!

After Snowy Fox had read her fill, she felt tired. She went upstairs to the bedroom and found the polar bears' three beds. Sleeping in beds! *Yes!* Her favorite! First, Snowy Fox tried papa polar bear's bed. *Ack.* It was much too hard. Next, she climbed into mama polar bear's bed. *Double ack.* It was way too fluffy. At last, she tried baby polar bear's bed, and *wow . . .* it was just right. Snowy Fox felt so comfy that she soon fell asleep.

A little while later, the polar bears returned from their walk. What a shock they had when they went to the kitchen and saw that nothing was as they had left it! The cabinet doors and drawers were hanging open, and food and pans had spilled out everywhere. Their bowls of porridge appeared to have moved as well.

"Somebody's been eating my porridge!" growled papa polar bear.

"And someone's been eating my porridge," said mama polar bear.

Baby polar pear started to cry when he saw his bowl. "Well, someone's been eating my porridge, too, and they ate it all gone!"

Next, the bears went to the living room and saw that someone had been messing around there, too.

"Somebody's been sitting in my chair!" growled papa polar bear.

"Someone's been sitting. in my chair and reading my new *Igloo Living,*" said mama polar bear.

Baby polar pear started to cry even harder when he saw his chair. "Well, someone's been sitting in my chair, too, and they broke it!"

The bears, who were pretty angry by this time, decided to go check out their bedroom to see if anyone had been there. Of course, someone had. The bears had made their beds neatly that morning, but now the covers were all mussed, and their pillows had been tossed about carelessly.

"Somebody's been sleeping in my bed!" growled papa polar bear.

"And someone's been sleeping in my bed," said mama polar bear.

Baby polar pear stopped crying when he saw his bed. "Well, someone's been sleeping in my bed, too, and there she is!"

At this, Snowy Fox awoke and sat up in baby polar bear's bed. At first, she couldn't remember where she was, but it all came back to her when she saw the three angry faces staring at her from across the room. *Uh-oh.* Angry polar bears! Snowy Fox was frightened half out of her wits. In fact, she was so scared that she shot up right out of the smoke hole in the igloo's roof. The polar bears ran outside to catch the intruder, but they could only watch as the speedy Snowy Fox tore away across the snow and ice.

From that day on, Snowy Fox never made an uninvited guest of herself in others' igloos. And even when she was invited, she never rifled through drawers, read magazines, or helped herself to so much as a crumb of sea salt without asking first.

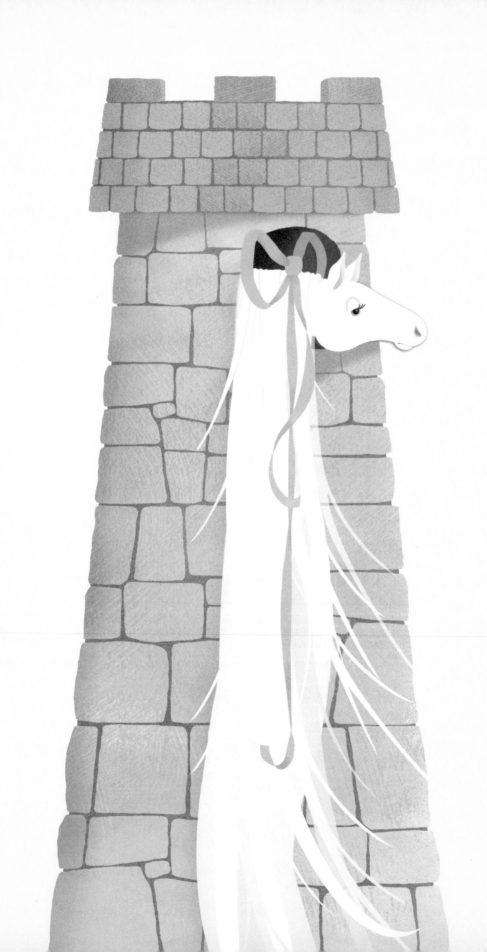

The Lonely Pony

There once lived a wicked snake enchantress who dreamed of having a pony of her very own. This is not to say that there's anything wrong with wanting a pony. Lots of us do. Pony wishes only become wicked when the wisher is willing to play mean tricks to get a pony and keep it all to herself.

Unfortunately, that's just what this old enchantress did.

One day, when she was out gathering herbs for her magic potions, the enchantress happened to pass the home of a pony couple out working in their garden. She saw that the pony wife was expecting a baby.

"Good morning," said the enchantress in her friendliest voice. "When will your baby be here? Soon?"

"Good morning," the pony wife replied. "The baby should arrive any day now."

"I see you have no carrots in your garden," said the enchantress. "A mother pony should have carrots to make her strong." The enchantress pulled a bunch of carrots from her basket. "Here, have some of mine."

"Thank you!" said the pony wife. "They look delicious, but let me trade you some beans or lettuces for them."

The enchantress smiled an oily smile. "Oh, no, no. The carrots are yours. Perhaps you can repay me another time. Good-bye."

With that, the enchantress slithered away, cackling to herself because she had put a spell on those carrots. Anyone who ate them would have to do whatever she commanded.

Three days later, the pony wife had her baby—a pretty little daughter as white as snow. What a shock it was when the new mother and father looked up from their baby's sweet face to find the old snake's face peering through the window!

"Oh, hello again," said the pony mother, recovering herself. "You're just in time to meet our new baby."

"*Yesssssss!*" hissed the enchantress, slipping inside. "And I've decided this is how you can repay me. Give your daughter to me."

The pony mother and father were horrified. They did not want to give away their baby, but because of the spell placed on the carrots they had eaten, they found that they could not disobey the enchantress. With a cackle, the old snake whisked the baby pony away and took her deep into the woods, where she placed her in a tall tower with no door, no stairs, and only a single small window.

Years passed, and the enchantress raised the pretty little pony as her own daughter. She fed her, played with her, and read her bedtime stories. But one thing the enchantress never did for her pony was let her out of the tower. Instead, the old snake preferred to keep her pony locked away so that she could brush her flowing mane whenever she wanted to. The enchantress even put a spell on the pony's mane so that it would never stop growing. Day by day, and year after year, the pony's white mane grew longer and longer.

In time, it grew long enough for the enchantress to use as a rope to slither up to the pony's window, high in the tower.

When she wanted to visit her pony, the enchantress would call, "Pretty pony, let down your mane!" And the pony would let down her long flowing locks and haul up the snake.

The little pony never thought to ask why she had a snake for a mother. She had never known any other. Still, there were other things the pony wondered about. She wondered what it would feel like to run free in the green grass below. She wondered if she was the only pony in the world, or if there were others . . . and if there were, could they be her friends? It would be nice to have a friend, she thought. The tower was such a lonely place.

One day, the pony decided to ask the snake her questions. "Mother," she said, for this was what she had always called the enchantress, "may I leave my tower and go run in the grass?"

"No, my dear," said the snake, "That wouldn't be safe at all."

Then the pony asked, "Mother, are there other ponies out there?"

"No, my darling," said the snake. "You are the only one, and that is why I must protect you. But look here. I've brought you some new blue ribbons. Let me tie them in your mane for you."

The innocent pony accepted these lies as truth, but she didn't feel any less lonely. In fact, she felt sadder than ever. It seemed like something was missing from her life, but she didn't know what it was. Even the pretty blue ribbons didn't cheer her up.

Three days later, the pony was sitting at her window, looking longingly at the grass and wildflowers outside. Suddenly, she noticed someone approaching. Whoever it was, they were running. It looked fun! The lonely pony soon saw that it was not the snake. This someone had four legs. When the stranger stopped below the lonely pony's window, she looked down and was surprised to see a pony much like herself, only brown, and with a much shorter mane.

"Hello, up there!" shouted the brown pony. "My name is Chocolate. Want to come for a run with me?"

The lonely pony was excited but also scared. "I'm not allowed," she shouted back, "and I'm not sure if I could get down even if I was."

"How odd," yelled Chocolate. "Every pony needs to run. But even if you can't leave, we can still talk, can't we?"

The lonely pony decided they could, and she and Chocolate enjoyed a nice long chat. It wasn't easy talking up and down like that. Even though they had to shout to hear each other, they were soon talking like old friends.

Chocolate promised to visit again the next day, and she was true to her word. She returned every day and told the lonely pony amazing things about the wide world. The lonely pony had never been happier.

One day, Chocolate told her, "You should meet my mother and father. They're the nicest ponies I know."

"You mean you have ponies for a mother and father?" asked the lonely pony.

"Of course!" said Chocolate.

"And they don't mind if you go outside?"

"Of course not!" said Chocolate. "I wish you could come down and meet them."

"I'd like to!" said the lonely pony. "Wait for me. I'm going to try to get down."

The lonely pony noticed the flagpole just outside her window, and she tossed the length of her mane over the pole. Chocolate saw what she meant to do, and clamped the long white mane firmly in her teeth. The lonely pony nodded and Chocolate let her down slowly and gently, using the mane as a pulley. It was working! But as soon as the lonely pony's hooves touched the ground, the two ponies heard a hiss behind them. Turning around, they found themselves face to face with the old snake enchantress herself! They might have run away from her, except that the lonely pony's long mane was twisted and caught around the flagpole high above.

"Stay where you are!" hissed the enchantress. "My pony must never leave me!"

"Yes, I'm afraid she must," said Chocolate, who had heard stories of snakes and their tricks. With that, Chocolate reared powerfully on her hind legs. Using the sharp edge of one of her horseshoes, she swung and cut clean through the lonely pony's long mane, freeing her from the tower once and for all.

When the lonely pony's mane was cut, the enchantress made a horrible sound. All her tricks and magic, all her wicked spells, went out of her. Through the years, she had wrapped all of her power up in that pretty mane to make it always grow. Now she had none. Chocolate and the lonely pony watched in amazement as the old snake faded and then disappeared completely.

The two ponies left the tower, and to the lonely pony, everything looked so new and exciting. The friends went on a thrilling run through the woods and to Chocolate's home to meet her mother and father. The old pony couple was overjoyed when they saw the pretty white pony they had heard so much about. Their hearts knew that this was the very daughter they had lost to the enchantress all those years ago. And the lonely pony, who was not so lonely anymore, felt in her heart that she had finally found what she had always been missing.

If you have enjoyed reading
these bedtime stories,
we would love to hear from you.

Please send your comments to:
Hallmark Book Feedback
P.O. Box 419034
Mail Drop 215
Kansas City, MO 64141

Or e-mail us at:
booknotes@hallmark.com